# GOODNIGHT MOON

## by Margaret Wise Brown
## Pictures by Clement Hurd

ISBN 0-590-09242-1

26                                                                        2 3/9

Printed in the U.S.A.                                                      08

SCHOLASTIC INC.
New York Toronto London Auckland Sydney

In the great green room
There was a telephone
And a red balloon
And a picture of—

**The cow jumping over the moon**

And there were three little bears sitting on chairs

And two little kittens
And a pair of mittens

And a little toyhouse
And a young mouse

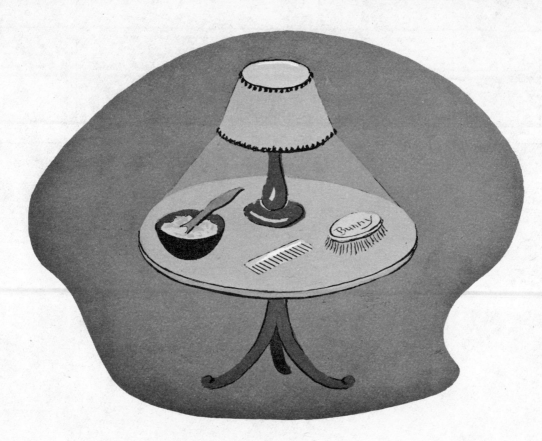

And a comb and a brush and a bowl full of mush

And a quiet old lady who was whispering "hush"

Goodnight room

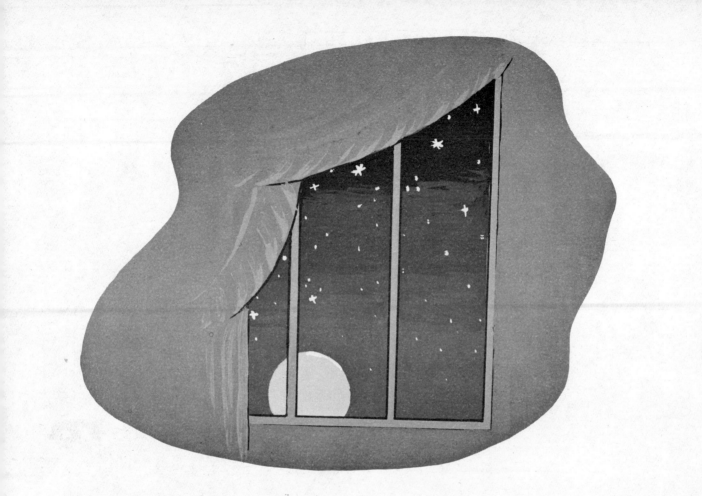

Goodnight moon

**Goodnight cow jumping over the moon**

Goodnight light
And the red balloon

Goodnight bears
Goodnight chairs

**Goodnight kittens**

**And goodnight mittens**

Goodnight clocks
And goodnight socks

**Goodnight little house**

And goodnight mouse

Goodnight comb
And goodnight brush

**Goodnight nobody**

Goodnight mush

And goodnight to the old lady
whispering "hush"

**Goodnight stars**

Goodnight air

Goodnight noises everywhere